This Orchard
book belongs to

DOG BISCUIT
DOG BISCUIT
DOG BISCUIT
DOG BISCUIT
DOG BISCUIT
DOG BISCUIT
DOG BISCUIT
DOG BISCUIT
DOG BISCUIT
DOG BISCUIT

DOG BISCUIT
DOG BISCUIT
DOG BISCUIT
DOG BISCUIT
DOG BISCUIT
DOG BISCUIT
DOG BISCUIT
DOG BISCUIT
DOG BISCUIT
DOG BISCUIT

For Anna Barcock
A true friend
With love from Emma

ORCHARD BOOKS
338 Euston Road, London NW1 3BH
Orchard Books Australia
Level 17/207 Kent Street, Sydney, NSW 2000

First published in 2008 by Orchard Books
First published in paperback in 2009

ISBN 978 1 84616 929 8

A CIP catalogue record for this book
is available from the British Library.

10 9 8 7 6 5 4 3 2 1

Printed in Singapore

Orchard Books is a division of Hachette Children's Books,
an Hachette Livre UK company.
www.hachettechildrens.co.uk

I don't want a posh dog
Emma Dodd
ORCHARD BOOKS

I don't
want
a posh
dog.

A blow-dry-when-washed dog.

I
don't
want a
patterned dog.
A jump-up-and-flatten

dog.

I don't want a handbag dog.

A tail-not-meant-to-wag dog.

I don't want

a snappy dog.

A growly,
never happy
dog.

I don't want
a gruff dog.

A grunty, wheezy,
puff dog.

I don’t want a

speedy dog.

A greedy,

weedy,

needy dog.

I don't want
an itchy dog.
A twitchy,
scratchy,
scritchy
dog.

I just want a silly dog.

A sweet, willy-nilly dog.

A not too proud or loud dog.

A know-me-in-the-crowd dog.

An
always keen
to try dog.

A dog I can call
My
Dog.

DOG BISCUIT
DOG BISCUIT
DOG BISCUIT
DOG BISCUIT
DOG BISCUIT
DOG BISCUIT
DOG BISCUIT
DOG BISCUIT
DOG BISCUIT
DOG BISCUIT

DOG BISCUIT
DOG BISCUIT
DOG BISCUIT
DOG BISCUIT
DOG BISCUIT
DOG BISCUIT
DOG BISCUIT
DOG BISCUIT
DOG BISCUIT
DOG BISCUIT

DOG BISCUIT